MY LITTLE GOLDEN
MOTHER GOOSE

Selected by
Robin Cohen

Illustrated by
Nan Brooks

A GOLDEN BOOK • NEW YORK

Golden Books Publishing Company, Inc., Racine, Wisconsin 53404

Old Mother Goose

—— ◆ ——

Old Mother Goose,
When she wanted to wander,
Would ride through the air
On a very fine gander.

Little Miss Muffet

— ◆ —

Little Miss Muffet
Sat on a tuffet,
Eating her curds and whey;
When along came a spider,
Who sat down beside her,
And frightened Miss Muffet away.

The Muffin Man

◆

Oh, do you know the muffin man,
The muffin man, the muffin man?
Oh, do you know the muffin man
Who lives in Drury Lane?

Humpty Dumpty

— ◆ —

Humpty Dumpty sat on a wall,
Humpty Dumpty had a great fall;
All the king's horses and all the king's men
Couldn't put Humpty Dumpty together again.

Butterfly, Butterfly

Butterfly, butterfly,
Whence do you come?
I know not, I ask not,
I never had a home.

Butterfly, butterfly,
Where do you go?
Where the sun shines, and
Where the buds grow.

Fiddle-De-Dee

Fiddle-de-dee, fiddle-de-dee,
The fly shall marry the bumblebee.
They went to church, and married was she;
The fly has married the bumblebee.

Bowwow, Says the Dog

——— ◆ ———

Bowwow, says the dog,
Mew, mew, says the cat,
Grunt, grunt, goes the hog,
And squeak goes the rat.

Tu-whu, says the owl,
Caw, caw, says the crow,
Quack, quack, says the duck,
And what the sparrows say, you know.

One, Two, Buckle My Shoe

◆

One, two, buckle my shoe;
Three, four, shut the door;
Five, six, pick up sticks;
Seven, eight, lay them straight;
Nine, ten, a good fat hen;
Eleven, twelve, dig and delve;
Thirteen, fourteen, maids are courting;
Fifteen, sixteen, maids in the kitchen;
Seventeen, eighteen, maids are waiting;
Nineteen, twenty, my platter's empty.

If

◆

If all the world were apple pie,
And all the sea were ink,
And all the trees were bread and cheese,
What would we have for drink?

I Sing, I Sing

—◆—

I sing, I sing
From morn till night;
From cares I'm free,
And my heart is light.

One I Love

—◆—

One I love, two I love,
Three I love, I say;
Four I love with all my heart,
Five I cast away.

I Saw a Ship A-Sailing

♦

I saw a ship a-sailing,
A-sailing on the sea;
And, oh! It was all laden
With pretty things for thee!

There were comfits in the cabin,
And apples in the hold;
The sails were made of silk,
And the masts were made of gold.

The four-and-twenty sailors
That stood between the deck
Were four-and-twenty white mice
With chains about their necks.

The captain was a duck
With a packet on his back;
And when the ship began to move,
The captain said, "Quack! Quack!"

Pussycat

—◆—

Pussycat, pussycat,
Where have you been?
"I've been to London
To look at the Queen."

Pussycat, pussycat,
What did you there?
"I frightened a little mouse
Under the chair."

There Was a Crooked Man

— ◆ —

There was a crooked man, and he went a crooked mile,
He found a crooked sixpence against a crooked stile;
He bought a crooked cat, which caught a crooked mouse,
And they all lived together in a little crooked house.

The Seasons

◆

Spring is showery, flowery, bowery;
Summer—hoppy, croppy, poppy;
Autumn—wheezy, sneezy, freezy;
Winter—slippy, drippy, nippy.

The North Wind

— ◆ —

The north wind doth blow,
And we shall have snow,
And what will the robin do then,
  Poor thing?

He'll sit in the barn
And keep himself warm,
And hide his head under his wing,
  Poor thing!

Little Boy Blue

— ◆ —

Little Boy Blue, come blow your horn!
The sheep's in the meadow, the cow's in the corn.
But where is the boy who looks after the sheep?
He's under the haystack, fast asleep.

The Cat and the Fiddle

— ◆ —

Hey, diddle, diddle,
The cat and the fiddle,
The cow jumped over the moon;
The little dog laughed to see such sport,
And the dish ran away with the spoon.

Old King Cole

——— ◆ ———

Old King Cole
Was a merry old soul,
And a merry old soul was he.

He called for his pipe,
And he called for his bowl,
And he called for his fiddlers three.

The Cats' Serenade

— ◆ —

The cats went out to serenade
And on a banjo sweetly played;
And summer nights they climbed a tree
And sang, "My love, oh, come to me!"

Daffy-down-dilly

— ◆ —

Daffy-down-dilly has come to town
In a yellow petticoat and a green gown.

There Was an Old Woman

— ◆ —

There was an old woman tossed up in a basket,
Seventeen times as high as the moon.
Where she was going I couldn't but ask it,
For in her hand she carried a broom.

"Old woman, old woman, old woman," said I,
"Where are you going up so high?"
"To sweep the cobwebs out of the sky!
And I'll be with you by-and-by."

Bedtime

— ◆ —

The Man in the Moon looked out of the moon
And this is what he said,
"'Tis time for all children on earth
To think about getting to bed!"

Twinkle, Twinkle, Little Star

— ◆ —

Twinkle, twinkle, little star!
How I wonder what you are,
Up above the world so high,
Like a diamond in the sky.